Four Adventure!

Four Short Stories
by
Sam Knight

Print Edition 2013
Knight Writing Press
KnightWritingPress@gmail.com

ISBN 978-1-62869-008-8

Published by

Knight Writing Press, an imprint of

Knight Writing LLC

Parker, CO 80134

knightwritingpress@gmail.com

Dedication

For my family, who tolerate me disappearing into my computer for hours, days, weeks at a time.

For my friends, who continue to help me, and more importantly, encourage me, when I need it the most.

Quincy J. Allen (http://www.quincyallen.com/)

Kevin J. Anderson and Rebecca Moesta (http://www.wordfire.com/)

David Boop (http://www.davidboop.com/)

J. A. Campbell (http://writerjacampbell.wordpress.com/)

Guy Anthony DeMarco (http://guyanthonydemarco.com/)

Pamela M. Nihiser (http://www.facebook.com/pamela.m.nihiser)

Kathryn Renta (http://www.kathrynrenta.com/)

Christopher M. Salas (https://www.facebook.com/CursesAndDemons)

For Peter J. Wacks (http://peterjwacks.com/)

For my critique group, be they No Name Heros, or be they part of the Cariboucrew, who will be sad to see I did not take all of their suggestions to heart.

For my Tribe, who can be found at http://www.authorfriends.com. If you are looking for a new author to try out, I know of no better place to start.

Four Adventure!

Gateway to the Garden of the Gods

"Are you sure about this?" Randy peered up nervously from the small dark hole beneath the giant sandstone formation. His hiking boots, khaki shorts, and white t-shirt matched Beth's close enough to have been planned that way. Above them towered the famous Kissing Camels of the Colorado Springs' Garden of the Gods, resplendently golden in the morning sunlight.

"Have I ever steered you wrong?" Beth stopped next to a small evergreen tree and threw back her shoulders to drop off her backpack, causing her chest to jut out as magnificently as the hogback rock formations around them.

The effect was not lost on Randy. Beth was in her prime with the golden skin tone, sun-bleached hair, and tight musculature of many hours spent in rugged country. A college student majoring in both geology and archaeology, she was proficient outdoors.

"No. You haven't steered me wrong—yet." Randy tried to keep his eyes on Beth's face as he spoke to her, "But we've only known each other for a couple of months. I'm sure you're still full of surprises."

"You got that right," she grinned at him slyly. "I might even surprise you a little somewhere down in that deep dark hole." She raised one eyebrow at Randy and his pulse quickened.

He watched her, entranced, as she pulled a light jacket out of her pack and put it on lithely. He realized she was preparing for the coolness of the cave and he glanced back at the hole with a grim look on his face. Once sealed with concrete, someone had attacked it with a hammer, exposing a jagged entrance. There was nothing else around to mark the place.

Beth had told him the history of Spaulding's Cave, sealed up by the City of Colorado Springs in 1935 and then again in 1963. People

3

had been arguing for opening it back up for several years, and now someone had apparently decided to take it upon themselves to do so. Beth wanted to take advantage of it while she could, before the Park realized it was open and sealed it again.

Randy sighed and dug out his own jacket while Beth fiddled with her camera. He was big on the idea of Beth, but not caving. Especially in a place he was sure they weren't supposed to be.

She had finally lured him here with his weakness—cryptozoology. He was a Bigfoot freak, spending his weekends and summers up in the mountains following recent reports of sightings and looking for tracks. That was how he met Beth.

They hooked up by chance at an impromptu campfire party when several groups of campers had shown up at the same spot in Phantom Canyon. He had been searching for recent signs of things alive, and she was searching for ancient traces of things long gone. She surprised him with a follow up phone call a week later. He thought she was way out the league of a lanky, curly-haired, nerd like himself, but a confluence of events and mutual interests had given him a chance with her and he was determined to make good on it.

So here he was. In the Garden of the Gods. Getting ready to follow the most beautiful woman he had ever dated into the depths of the earth searching for GOG, the Garden of the Gods monster. Illegally. And she had hinted at sex in the cave.

His stomach knotted with nervous excitement. One way or another, this would be a day to remember, that was for sure.

Beth caught him staring at her and grinned. She shrugged her backpack onto her shoulders. "Ready?" she asked.

Randy nodded and put on his hat with the headlamp and helmet-cam strapped to it. "You want to go first?"

"So you can get close ups of my ass with that camera while I wiggle through that hole? No thank you. You first. I want to be the one with the view." She winked at him salaciously.

"Okay. But explain to me about this cave one more time." Randy put on his pack.

"Again?" she frowned.

"It'll take my mind off doing something I know I shouldn't be doing," he explained. "Besides, I like the sound of your voice."

"All right," she shrugged. As she talked he climbed to the top of the cement rubble and peeked in. "I was researching Theiophytalia kerri, a dinosaur named after the Garden of the Gods because the only fossil of it, a skull, was found here in the Park."

4

This wasn't the part of the story Randy was interested in. He ignored her speech as he scraped his belly across a wicked piece of rebar and thrust his head into the damp darkness, grateful for being so skinny.

"I was talking to a grad student about places to look for fossils when he told me he knew someone who had been in Spaulding's Cave recently." Beth's voice muffled as Randy snaked into the hole. "I knew about the names and dates carved into the walls by people who had visited here hundreds of years ago," Beth grunted as she pulled herself up to follow Randy, "and that in the Sixties they hauled out seventy-five truckloads of dirt to dig down and expose the walls, where even more carvings had been buried as sediment fell over time."

The air was damp and cool with a stale smell to it. Water dripped somewhere in the darkness. As he finished pulling himself in on his stomach, Randy's headlamp illuminated stairs, carved out of the sandstone, leading downwards in front of his face. There were boot tracks in the sediment on the steps. And a hand print right where he was about to place his own hand. Whoever had been here hadn't been a little kid.

"But this grad student said there was more than just names on the walls. He said there were cave paintings, too. And I want to make sure I get to see them before it gets sealed up again." Beth struggled in the hole. Although she was considerably more petite than Randy, her chest and hips didn't slide through as easily.

"I don't know why no one mentions the cave paintings in the records of the cave." She struggled for a moment to unhook a belt loop caught on the rebar that had scraped Randy. Then Randy caught her hands and helped her the rest of the way through, trying not to shine his headlamp into her eyes.

When Beth was able to stand, she brushed herself off and giggled. "Isn't this exciting?" she whispered and gave Randy a quick kiss on the lips before moving past him, down the roughhewn stairs.

He mentally agreed as he smiled and followed, trying not to let the helmet-cam linger on her butt.

She forgot to finish her story, but he had already heard it. Some of the cave paintings supposedly showed large hairy men, and that was what interested him. Years ago, while researching GOG, Randy had found a reference to an Indian legend about the Garden of the Gods. Giants, taller than trees, with ground-shaking footsteps, had invaded the land along with fearsome creatures, but Manitou, the protector of the people, had turned them to stone. They still stood, as giant rocks, creating the place now called the Garden of the Gods.

The scuff of their boots on the rock steps seemed to echo louder than the original sound and Randy thought he could even hear their breathing echo. Mere feet from the entrance they had crawled through, they entered a long narrow chamber, shaped like a hall extending off to both the left and the right. The far wall was only about ten feet away, but their lights shone off into darkness without finding either end of the hallway. He looked up, surprised to see the ceiling was at least seventy feet overhead.

"Look!" Beth's exclamation thundered through the cavern causing her and Randy to both flinch in surprise. Dust fell in the beams of their headlamps, shaken loose by the vibrations.

"I think we should whisper," Randy whispered. The echo still came back as loud as someone talking.

"Yeah," Beth agreed even quieter. "Look," she repeated herself at the barest whisper, yet Randy could hear her easily. Her headlamp shone on a name carved into the sandstone. W. Jackson. Under it was the date, 1870. As Randy turned to look, his light added to Beth's, revealing many names and dates etched into the soft sandstone. The oldest they spotted was 1858.

"How did they reach up so high?" Randy asked, looking at names ten feet up.

"The dirt was higher then, remember? Seventy-five truckloads of dirt came out of here in the Sixties." Beth readied her camera and snapped a photo. "I wish I knew where they dumped it. The archaeological value could have been huge!"

The reflection of the camera flash on the wall blinded Randy and he moved away to avoid the next one.

Examining the damp sandy floor, he concluded that water must flow through occasionally, leaving patterns resembling a small dry creek bed. He chose to go left at random and moved further into the darkness, following the boot prints of the person who had been in the cave before.

As Beth's camera flashed again, he saw the passage way lit for an instant and was astounded to realize most of the Kissing Camels hogback had to be hollow. He moved further back and found that parts of the cavern were enormous, up to a hundred feet high. After a hundred feet or so he found the end of the hallway and signs of the work done fifty-some years earlier. A broken shovel handle, a matted leather glove, and a Coke bottle. The wall looked like water ran down it here, and it was cold and wet to the touch.

Looking around, he found nothing else, so he headed back towards Beth, keeping his eyes on the walls or the ground to avoid her camera flash. As he passed her, she stopped taking pictures and pinched his butt.

"Thank you so much for coming with me," she whispered, "I really appreciate it."

"I suspect you could talk me into most anything," he confessed, hoping she didn't realize how true of a statement it was.

She smiled and turned back to take more photos of the names. As her light flooded the room again, a strange mark on the wall caught his eye. It cornered around the entrance and into the hall of the cave.

He moved to look at the dark mark. It was an odd straight line, sharp and defined along the bottom edge then fading at the top. He followed it down the passage until it faded away, and then he followed it back. It only ran a couple of feet from the corner in either direction.

Randy touched the black stuff and some came off on his fingers. The pattern looked like the marks left on cement after lighting a fuse on fireworks. Had they blasted in here? Maybe to hurry the excavating process?

He worked his way farther into the cavern. The floor was barren, except for the boot prints, and no one had seemed to feel the need to carve their name on the wall this far into the cave. The tracks helped him find the cave painting. Boot prints mulled all around where someone had stood and looked at it. Randy was enraptured.

Unlike any cave painting he had seen before, this one was both painted and carved into the sandstone. And it obviously showed something that looked like a Bigfoot.

He pulled out his camera and for a moment his flashes joined Beth's, filling the cavern like strobe lights.

Beth noticed Randy's camera flashes, and curiosity got the better of her. She moved carefully through the darkness, following his flashes like a lighthouse beacon, until she got close enough to see the pictograph.

"I've never seen anything like it," she whispered.

"I'm no expert," Randy whispered back, "but my guess is this is a warning that has been added onto several times over the centuries."

"I've studied some cave paintings, but this is like a blend of different cultures, different peoples. It looks like a great battle is represented here, between men and ... these things." She pointed to a dark humanoid figure that towered twice as tall as the men represented with bows and arrows.

"I agree. This has to be a warning. The dismembered bodies and skulls are pretty much a universal symbol. I think this is the outside of this cave." What she pointed to didn't look exactly like the Kissing Camels formation, but rather how they may have appeared centuries earlier.

"What do you think these are?" Beth asked, pointing out large quadrupeds.

"At first I thought they were bison, but look at this." Randy pointed at one of the four-legged creatures trampling a man. The beast was represented twice as tall as the man, and its long horns were each nearly as long as the man. "That is just too big for bison. And look at this." He pointed to another monster. With a face like a bear, it stood on two legs and had huge claws on the ends of its hands and feet. "I know what this one is. This is a giant sloth."

"A sloth?" Beth came over for a better look.

"Yeah. I think we are looking at drawings of prehistoric mega-fauna. The giant animals that roamed the earth after the dinosaurs and before man."

"Not so much before man if that's what this is showing," Beth corrected him.

Randy nodded. "This would be a huge find. To prove that man existed with some of these creatures would really back up the theory that we killed them off, not climate changes." He pointed back to one of the giant hairy men. "But this is what interests me the most."

"Yeah, yeah. Mr. Bigfoot." Beth playfully bumped Randy with her hip.

"Well, yeah. If these are real creatures," he pointed at the giant bison, the sloth, a couple of things that looked like bears, and one that resembled a rhinoceros with strange flat horns on its face, "then these must be real, too." He moved his finger back to the hairy men.

"So you think this proves Bigfoot is real?"

"No. But these could be Gigantopithecus. They have only been found in China, India, and Viet Nam. This could prove they were here, and that makes it even more possible that Bigfoot is real."

"Aren't you glad you came?" Beth whispered and moved further into the tunnel to see if there was more.

"You bring me to all the best places," Randy whispered back and followed her.

They reached the end of the cavern. A pile of rocks, boulders, sand, and gravel prevented them from going any further. The boot prints Randy had been following turned back here also. There were no other cave drawings.

"I guess that's it," Beth mumbled.

"I guess so. Still, this is much more than I thought could be hidden here. I'm going to take some more photos and video of the drawing, just to make sure it all turns out."

"What's that?" Beth asked and pointed to marks on one of the boulders filling the end of the passage.

Randy bent to look at the hole drilled into the rock. "That's for blasting. They drill the holes to control what breaks and falls out. I saw fuse burns back there on the wall. They must have been trying to open this up or something when they hauled out all those truckloads of dirt. I wonder if they were looking for another Cave of the Winds ..." Randy's voice trailed off as he thought about it. He headed back towards the entrance to look at the burns again.

"There were rumors that this cave connected to the cave systems up by the Cave of the Winds, but I read that was impossible, geologically speaking," Beth offered as she followed him.

"Why would they have used a burning fuse in the Sixties?" Randy mused as he stopped and looked at the burn marks on the wall.

"What?"

"Here," he pointed. "This is from a burning fuse. Why didn't they use electric blasting caps?"

"Look how high up they are," Beth pointed out. "Wouldn't the fuse have lain on the ground? I bet this is from before they took out the dirt."

"You're right. I bet blasting has happened in here more than once." Randy furrowed his brow again. "How much of that pictogram do you suppose was buried before they hauled out the dirt?"

"If this fuse line is any indication, I would guess at least half." Beth used her hand on her hip to mark the height of the fuse line and then headed back to the cave drawing. "If the fuse line is a good indicator, and if they took the dirt out evenly, I'd say enough was buried to prevent it from being recognized as a warning, that's for sure. All that would have been visible was this stuff up here." She waved her hand at something that looked like brown rivers drawn above the rest of the pictogram.

Randy stepped closer and looked at them with her. "I wonder what those are supposed to be? They look like roads or paths. See these? They look like figures walking on them. And here, and here, it looks like the people who went that way died. I wonder if this could be a map of a tunnel system." He turned to look at Beth.

9

Beth wasn't paying attention to him, she was had climbed part way up the wall of boulders at the end of the cave and was waving her hand around curiously.

"What are you doing?" Randy asked.

"I feel a breeze coming from here. I think you're right. I think it's a map of a tunnel system, and if they had just bothered to clear this out after the last time they blasted, they would have found it!" She climbed up the rubble a little ways and began pulling at rocks.

"Don't do that!" Randy hissed. "It's not stable!"

"Come on!" Beth hissed back. "This could be the discovery of a lifetime!"

"Get off it, Lois Lane! That's dangerous! Seriously!" A large rock came free and tumbled down at Randy's feet.

"I can see in! They were so close it's unbelievable! There's a passage back here! I think I can squeeze in!" Beth started pushing herself through even as she spoke.

"Beth! Damn it! We don't have any equipment for that! Don't go in there!" She was through before Randy could finish.

Randy climbed up to look into the hole Beth had gone into. "Beth?" he called as he stuck his head in. "Are you okay?"

"Holy shit, Randy! You've gotta see this! Get in here!" Beth could hardly hold in her excitement. "Look at this!"

Randy stuck his head in the hole and began worming through. Rocks had fallen and supported themselves to make a tunnel about five feet long. He fit easily and came through quickly. As he righted himself, his eyes were drawn to an object, in Beth's hands, spotlighted by her headlamp.

She was holding a skull. It appeared to be human, but it was twice the size of Beth's head as she held it up and peered into its empty sockets.

"I think I have your proof," she murmured as he approached. She turned her head to illuminate the rest of the skeleton on the ground. It was enormous, proportioned like a man who would have stood close to ten feet tall.

"Look at this." She turned her head and aimed the light at the sediment on the ground further into the passage. It had been packed down from the weight of many footsteps, one of which was clearly visible and nearly double the size of Randy's own prints. Randy stepped over to it, amazed.

"I think we found evidence of Bigfoot, what do you think?" Beth asked him. Her eyes glittered brightly in the darkness.

Randy grinned uncontrollably. He pulled out his camera and began snapping photos. Beth, holding the skull out so he could use her as a size reference, posed stylishly and blew him kisses.

"Let's put the skull back so I can take some shots of where it was," Randy directed her.

She placed it with the rest of the skeleton and he moved in to take pictures.

"These footprints have to have been made since they closed the cave." Randy observed as he moved to take pictures of the prints. "All of the footprints in the other part have been erased by falling dust. How old do you think these could be?"

"Well it took less than fifty years to completely obliterate the other prints, and these still look fresh, so I would guess these could be anywhere from hours old up to ten or twenty years. Probably a lot less than twenty years. There really isn't a dust build up here where the dirt has been packed. It's almost like this gets walked on regularly."

As his flash lit up the area again, something farther into the cave caught Beth's eye, reflecting the light. Twin somethings. Two orbs flashing when Randy's camera flashed.

"Randy." Her voice caught in her throat as she backed towards him. "Randy!" She hissed.

"Yeah?"

"Eyes! Eyes!" She backed into him and he turned to see the twin reflections shining at them out of the dark. He caught her by the shoulders and held tight as he backed up with her until he began slipping on the rubble pile.

"You go first!" He pushed her up towards the exit without looking away. As she climbed, he watched their watcher.

"Wait!" He stopped her just as she was about to go out.

"What?" her voice trembled.

"Stay here. It's not moving. I don't think it's alive." Randy began moving slowly towards the eyes.

"Randy! No! Come back here!"

"Gee, that sounds familiar, doesn't it?" He chided her as he moved closer to the glowing orbs. Nothing seemed to change.

Beth cursed and continued hissing at him, but he ignored her. As he moved closer, the reflections came into focus. "Oh my God. Beth! Get over here!"

Randy's light revealed the empty sockets of a skull wearing glasses. The skull had been carefully placed into a small recess in the cave wall. Next to it were a dozen or more skulls, each with their own

11

resting place carved into the wall. Rings, watches, coins and various other things rested in the alcoves with the skulls.

Beth came up behind him, and he could hear her breathing as she tried to take it in.

"I don't think that is hundreds of years old." Randy pointed to an old-fashioned walkie-talkie leaning against one of the skulls. "In fact, I'd guess it's from around Nineteen-Sixty."

"Could they have been trapped in a cave-in?" Beth gripped Randy's arm without realizing it.

Randy shook his head. "You saw how easily we got in here. If they had been trying to get out, they would have made it. The passage you found was blocked from view on that side, but it's easy to see on this side."

Randy raised his camera and snapped a picture of the skulls. One of them caught Beth's attention and she examined it closer. It had bite marks on it, scrapes on the bone caused by teeth. She looked at the next one. And the next. They were all like that. They had all been ... eaten clean.

"Oh, shit," Beth breathed as the realization washed over her. "We have to get out of here."

"They're long dead, don't worry about it."

"No, you don't get it. We have to get out of here!" Beth grabbed his arm and started pulling him backwards.

"Hey!" Randy momentarily forgot to whisper and the sound echoed loudly through the tunnel.

"They weren't blasting to get in!" Beth hissed as she pulled him behind her. "They were blasting it shut! Whatever happened here, they covered it up, and they meant for it to stay covered up!"

Randy started to argue with her but a distant echoing groan froze them both. Randy felt the hair on his neck stand up. His stomach knotted, and he felt himself start to panic in a way he had never experienced before—a primal reaction to a racial memory of a predator that hunted man.

"Go! Go! Go!" He turned and pushed Beth towards the rubble pile. She scrambled up as Randy pushed from behind. Something was coming.

Beth squirmed into the hole, scraping her knees and elbows, moving as fast as she could. Randy pushed from behind trying to help and then she was through, falling out the other side, down the rock pile. She turned to help pull Randy through, but there was no sign of his headlamp coming through the hole.

"Randy?" Beth climbed back up and tried to see into the hole. "Randy!" There was no sign of him. Beth panicked. "RANDY!" she screamed.

The echoes bounced off the walls, shaking loose dust and dirt. She screamed again, but only her echoes answered.

"Randy!" She screamed a final time as rocks broke loose and crashed somewhere distantly in the cave. A deep rumbling sound filled her senses and she yelped as a dark figure popped through the hole out of the darkness and bowled her over.

They tumbled down the rocks together, then Randy was pulling her up and running for the cave exit. Beth tried to keep facing forward so they could see by the light of her headlamp, but her light swung wildly. Finally they reached the hole, and Randy shoved her through the concrete opening, mindless of the rebar. He scrambled after her, falling to the ground next to her, and they both lay panting and squinting at the bright morning sun.

A deep rumble came from within the cave and they jumped up and moved away quickly.

"What happened? Why didn't you answer me?" Beth hit him on the chest with frustrated fury and relief, tears shining in her eyes.

"I had to toss my headlamp to distract it. I had to give you more time to get out. It was right on top of us."

Beth wrapped her arms around him and cried. After a minute she pulled away and wiped her eyes.

"Next time," she poked him in the chest, "we come prepared."

Plunder on the High Sands

The Sahara
1692

The sharp pain of cracking dry lips woke the man known as Spits. He winced at the bright glare that hurt his head and ruined his eyes. Putting up a hand up to block the demon sun brought agony to his wrist. Sand fell into his eyes from the ragged folds of his sleeves, adding to the pain.

Miserably, he sat up and found the burning sand too hot for the palms of his dirty hands. Looking at the painful rope burns on his wrists, he wondered how they had gotten there, even before he realized he had no idea where he was.

An endless sea of sand loomed all around him, reflecting the hot yellow of the sun from everywhere but the blue sky.

Spits righted himself and found the sand burned his bare feet unless he stood where he had been lying. Standing did not improve his view.

The hateful ball of fire above him was high enough he couldn't guess any bearings from it. The only landmarks were high dunes to his right and, to his left, mountains so faint he could hardly see them.

He tried to curse, but his throat was too dry, his tongue too swollen. Moving his tongue to work up spit in his mouth failed to do anything but cause more pain.

The dagger he usually wore in his rope belt was missing. As was the belt, all seven of the gold rings he had worn in his ears, and everything else he owned—except the ragged pants and shirt he had stolen from the corpse of Captain Percival H. Cox of the HMS Bucknowle in an alley behind a whore house in Punta Gorda.

He looked around and found what he believed to be tracks leading to and away from where he had awakened, but in the sand he couldn't guess which way was which.

He was at a loss for what to do. His life was the sea, not this barren Hell.

Hell ...

Had he died? His last memory was of drink and watching the smooth brown belly of a Moroccan beauty in Casablanca, a dancer covered in shimmering silk and lust. He could remember nothing more.

Obviously his feet and hands had been bound. He had seen the same sores on many slaves. Had slavers taken him? Why was he untied now? Where was he? The sunburn on his arms and the blisters on his face and the top of his feet told him he had been here too long already.

Spits chose at random and began following the tracks, not knowing if it was the way they had come from or gone. The sand shifted and was difficult to walk on. It ate at his callused heels and scalded the tops of his feet. He made no more than ten steps before tripping and falling from exhaustion.

A pathetic wail of despair escaped his lips. Either he was in Hell and this was his fate for all eternity, or he would die here, not knowing how or why he had come to this place. The heat of the desert was too much for direct contact with his skin and he got to his knees to keep his arms out of the burning sand.

It occurred to him to pray, but he did not know how.

A sharp whistle pierced his despair, and he looked around quickly. From behind him, a figure riding a camel approached, silhouetted against the dune it had come over. The whistle came again and he recognized it as a call to grog at the end of a shift. His mouth puckered at the thought, anticipating liquids, but unable to salivate.

The figure waved and Spits recognized the man as one of his own crew, an uppity bastard they called Prince, who was allowed to wear only burlap after the Captain took insult to him.

How's and why's Prince should come to be here were far from his mind as a grin split his lips and made them bleed. He waived back with renewed energy and managed to get to his feet again.

When Prince was close enough to be heard he called out, "I told them you had a spit left in you yet, but they were too busy pulling off gold rings to listen. It was like they wanted you to be dead."

Spits tried to answer but couldn't, his throat only rasped.

The camel belched as Prince reached Spits and tossed him a wineskin. Spits fumbled with it and began shaking as he prepared to pour the blessed liquid into his mouth.

"Go slow, or it will hurt you as bad as not having any," Prince advised as the camel kneeled and he slid off.

Spits cried as he got little more than a mouthful from the now empty skin. He swished the weak wine mixed with water around in his mouth, relishing the wetness, the stinging on his tongue and cracked lips, the flavor that wasn't dust.

He tried to talk again but still couldn't. The liquid hadn't helped the swelling of his tongue.

"They are all just over that dune, camped under a big tent," Prince assured him. "Sure will be nice to get back to it and get out of the sun."

"More ..." Spits finally managed to beg, holding out the empty wineskin.

Prince nodded. "I've got more." He pulled another from the camel's pack but made no move to hand it to Spits. "But it will cost you."

Anger flashed in Spits' eyes as he looked into the swarthy man's face.

"Come now," Prince grinned slyly at him and spread his arms wide, "they left you for dead. I'm the only one who came back to see if you were alive. Surely I deserve something for that!"

Spits tried to say something but could still hardly croak. Prince tossed him the wineskin. "On your honor, then," he told Spits and sat down in the shade of the kneeling camel.

"Sit here next to me, in the shade." Prince patted the sand then pulled off his makeshift burlap shirt to mop at his face. "Blasted sun! Pulls the life right from your skin!"

Spits eyed him warily before stumbling into the shade. He sat down gratefully, struggling to open the new wineskin with unresponsive fingers.

"I know what your wondering. You want to know why lowly Prince would risk his own skin to come back for the ever-hated Spits."

Spits looked at him sharply.

"Admit it, you know everyone hates you. The only friend you've made in the last ten years was the Captain." Prince looked around exaggeratedly, "And where is he? Did he come back for you?" Prince grinned widely. "All right. I admit I have a motive. Two of them. Do you remember the first time we met? No? Well think on it while I tell you my second reason."

Prince leaned in and whispered. "I want you to tell me where the Captain keeps the charts marked with the caches."

Spits slowly swished the liquid around in his mouth before swallowing.

The Captain would gut both of them if he even suspected this kind of talk. Then again, the Captain hadn't come back, had he?

Spits eyed the ragged dark skinned man in front of him and tried to remember the first time they had met.

It had been in the hold of the ship, he was sure. That was where Spits met with all of the new 'recruits'.

"On yer feet!" Spittle flew from the fat ugly lips of the Quartermaster known, appropriately, as Spits. Spits kicked at the limp forms of the drugged men who had been brought aboard in the dead of night nearly two days before.

He grabbed a bucket of wash and began slinging the water around on the men, taking a perverse delight in knowing the salt water would make them even thirstier than their stupor had.

"On yer feet! Ye work here, or ye go overboard! And it is time to work!" He kicked at one of the men. There were five this time, more than usual. Too many became hard to control, but as many as six had been done before.

"Please, Sir? Where am I?" One of the men asked meekly.

"Ach!" Spits spat. It was no good to have men as weak as this one sounded. "Yer in Hell! And yer master has called you to work! Get up!" He kicked at the dark skinned man. Moroccan, he guessed, maybe Indian.

"Please, I can pay you. I'm Prince..."

One of the other recruits began vomiting profusely and Spits roared with laughter. "What a name! Ho! I wonder what that means in the King's English! Ho! Ho!"

Spits called up the stairs and a big man quickly came down. "Go fetch another bucket o' brine and a swab so Prince here can get busy with his first assignment!" He jerked a thumb at the mess and laughed again, moving on to kick at another man who had not yet moved.

"Prince ..." Spits rasped. "Ye told me ye be a prince."

Prince nodded. "That I did. Take another mouthful. You are doing well with your restraint."

Spits took another drink and Prince smiled at him. "I am a prince, you know. My people are called the Dom. Some call us gypsies. We are a traveling people. Nomads. Traders." He looked wistful. "Anyway. As I thought of you lying here, dying, it occurred to me that, as far as I know, only you and the Captain know where the caches are. And if anything happened to you, then it would only be the Captain." He scratched his jaw thoughtfully. "Then I started to wonder if you had any family. Obviously, you have helped earn no small part of the Captain's fortune. Would he send your share to your family? No. I thought not. Not after you were left here to die. Stripped even of your earrings without so much as the burial they were to pay for. Left like extra chum floating behind a full ship. Useless. Unthought-of. Uncared for."

Prince watched Spits to let the thought sink in before continuing. "Then I said to myself, 'if he can still tell me where the caches are, I might be able to get his share to his family someday. If he has any family.' Do you have any family?"

Spits shook his head.

"Ah well. Come on!" Prince stood up and held a hand out for Spits. "We should rejoin the caravan before they move out and lose us."

"Caravan?" Spits asked.

"Aye. We're in the desert." He helped Spits onto the camel and then goaded the creature to its feet. "Oh I forgot. You were so delirious you probably don't know what's going on. I'll let the Captain explain it to you." Prince smirked and pointed at his own burlap clothing. "I'd not upset him again soon! But I'll tell you this; it has to do with some deal with slavers."

Prince caught the camel's rope lead and began walking back the way he had come.

Spits rocked unsteadily on the beast as he looked down at the top of Prince's head. "Ye really came back for me?"

"Aye."

They rode in silence to the top of the dune. As they crested, Spits could make out a small camp of tents and a group of people not too far in the distance.

"That must be the slavers!" Prince called over his shoulder and pointed to a line of camels, wagons and people merging with the camp. "It's about time!"

Spits' spirits rose at the signs life, of people. He wasn't in Hell after all. He wasn't going to die here. He felt giddy.

"Prince?" he called.

"Aye?"

"Ye gave me payment on me honor."

"Aye."

"The charts be in a hollowed out plank under the Captain's bunk. If anything ever happens to me ... again. Ye keep me share for yerself!" He sat high on the camel experiencing a feeling he didn't recognize.

Prince stopped the camel and looked back up at Spits for a long moment before nodding and continuing on to the camp.

When they arrived, they were surrounded by dark men who greeted Prince eagerly and slapped him on the arms and back. The words they spoke moved too fast and fluidly for Spits, even had they been in his own language. Hands caught at Spits and pulled him gently down from the camel and led him into the shade of the tents.

The tents were stretched out, covering several wagons, providing shade for the men sitting in them. His crew, Spits realized. The familiar faces wore unfamiliar expressions, and many of them called to him, but the chatter of all the people around him drowned out anything he might have heard. He looked for the Captain, but didn't see him. He must be meeting with the leader of the slavers, Spits thought.

A sharp pain in his wrist made him gasp and, as he turned to see what had happened, his other arm was grabbed. Nearly instantly his hands were bound behind his back. The pain of the bindings on the raw rope burns made him cry out, but his cries went unheeded as he was lifted and tossed into one of the wagons.

"Ye rotten bastard, Spits!" A foot caught him on the ear as hard as a shackled foot could.

As he felt shackles locking upon his own ankles, he saw the kicker was a recruit from two ports ago. The foot came at him again and he twisted to avoid it, doing his best to sit up in the wagon.

Prince appeared then, with a man dressed in flowing white robes at his elbow. They exchanged words Spits couldn't follow, and then Prince turned to look at him. "Spits, this is Sheikh Kalar, your new owner. I have asked him to take special care of you and treat you appropriately."

Realization set in and spittle flew as Spits yelled at Prince, "I gave ye what ye wanted! Backstabber!"

"I told you I had two motives. Do you remember the first time we met?" Prince smiled grimly and walked away.

"Ye bastard!" Spits cried out. He remembered now. It hadn't been in the hold. The first time they met had been in a tavern, over a pint. Prince had asked Spits what life was like out at sea. Spits had promised to show him as he had drugged Prince's mug.

"You'll rot in Hell!" Spits cried. "In Hell!"

Prince stopped and walked back. "I already did," he hissed. "Now it's your turn."

Four Adventure!

Old Snorter

Colorado
1891

"Damnation! Look at the size of that sumbitch!"

Gable grimaced, irritated at the sound of Parker's hissed words.

The little man continued whispering without taking his eyes off the buck. "It's big as an elk!"

The mule deer stood on the mountain across the gulch below, nearly three hundred yards away, looking at the two men standing next to their four horses. The buck's rack carried eight points on either side. It didn't move. Not even an ear twitch.

"See 'im?" Parker asked, still looking around the neck of the packhorse he had been unloading.

"I see. Why don't you shoot him?" Gable chuckled to himself as he admired the animal.

"You know my baby ain't got that kind of range." Parker gave the big red-headed man a sideways look. The two men had been arguing over the value of Parker's new .22 pump action rifle for the last two weeks.

This was the first time the men had gone out together, and Gable had quickly regretted his choice of companion. Not only did the little man's incessant talking and complaining grate on him, but they were a week out of where Gable thought they ought to be, and he was irritated at Parker's insistence on coming all the way out here. Tension between the two men had started to come out in the little things—like the usefulness of Parker's gun.

With Parker's admission that his rifle couldn't make the shot, Gable grunted in satisfaction and eased his own Hawken .50 caliber out of his saddle holster, laying it across the back of his horse. Other than the distance, he couldn't ask for a better shot.

The buck still stared at them across the valley, unmoving and perfectly silhouetted in the middle of a melting patch of snow.

Gable whispered to his horse, letting it know he was about to fire. A good trail horse, it held still as he aimed across its saddle and pulled the set trigger, readying the rifle for a shot. He exhaled and pulled the second trigger. The muzzleloader cracked the silence of the piney forest and a plume of blue smoke drifted from where the hammer had dropped. One of the pack horses startled, but it was tethered to Gable's horse and unable to pull away from the better trained animal.

"Hooeey! You dropped him like a rock! That was a hell of a shot." Parker slapped his hat on his leg in excitement. "We ain't eating no sonofabitch stew tonight!" He grinned wide, his greasy black hair plastered to his head.

Gable grinned wryly, satisfied he had shown up the little man's rifle. His right eye watered from the powder smoke as he squinted at the empty snowy patch. "I don't see him."

"He din't go nowheres. He fell like a sack of taters."

Gable kept his eyes on the spot while he poured more gunpowder down the barrel of his rifle. He thought he had made a good shot, but it bothered him he couldn't see the carcass in the snow. He used the ramrod to push the patch and ball down into the Hawken, but still nothing moved. A good sign he had made a clean kill.

"Here," he handed the muzzleloader to Parker once he was done placing a new firing cap under the hammer. "Let me take your Winchester in case I didn't get him clean."

"What, that Colt on yer hip ain't good enough? Oh, I see. You wanna hold my girl for a while." Parker winked and pulled his new Winchester rifle out of its holster. "You treat her right, and don't forget she goes home with me at night." He traded rifles with Gable. "She ain't no one-shot whore. I paid more'n twenty dollar for her."

"Walk me in." Gable ignored the jibe and started towards the kill. Parker's rifle felt light and fragile in his oversized hands. He lumbered down the rocky slope into the scrub oak marking the wash between the mountains. Dried leaves and branches crackled and snapped with his passing as he scraped through.

"You a noisy bastard, ain't cha?" He heard Parker laughing at him. "Good thing they ain't no injuns 'round her no more, or they'd have your scalp for sure!"

Gable wondered if Indians wouldn't shoot the idiot yelling first. He came out of the thicket on the far slope and turned to look back. Parker had begun repacking the horses. Gable approved of the man's actions for a change. It would be easier to bring the horses to the kill than it would be to drag the carcass all the way back. He whistled to get Parker's attention.

Parker looked up at Gable, then took his hat off and held it straight up in the air with his skinny arm.

Gable turned and kept walking up the mountain, working his way around a large boulder pile and then backtracking when he was blocked by a dense growth of trees. Back around the boulder pile, he stopped and turned for directions again.

Parker held his hat out to the right and Gable moved that way until he found the patch of snow.

Gable walked a circle around the snow patch. There were no tracks, no blood. He walked the snow patch again, this time in a wider circle. Nothing. There was no sign of the buck.

He whistled again. Parker turned to look at him and Gable spread his arms wide.

"It's right there, idjit!" Parker hollered across the draw. He took off his hat again, waving it in a circle to tell Gable he was already there. Gable walked one more circle around the snow patch and stopped with his arms spread wide again.

Parker flopped his arms down at his sides with over-exaggerated exasperation and waved his hat again. "Just look for the damn tracks already!"

Gable dropped his arms and began walking back to camp, ignoring Parker's waving hat.

"You don't like where he fell? We need to find another one to shoot?" Parker paced, irritated, as Gable approached.

"There's nothing there," Gable answered. "You walk me into the right patch of snow?"

They both looked back at the mountain. There was only one patch of snow.

Parker shook his head in disgust. "You take the horses and meet me up there."

Gable shrugged and passed off the repeating rifle as the skinny man went by him in a huff. He tried hard to keep his own annoyance off his face. Not for the first time, Gable wondered why he had paired off with Parker.

He watched Parker walk up the mountain and around the patch of snow. Parker stepped out into the snow. His boots sunk readily into the melting snow. Walking to the center of the white patch, he turned around in a circle, looking. He took of his hat, scratched his head angrily, and cursed at the sky. "I know you was right here, you sumbitch!"

His reedy voice carried back and Gable smirked at his frustration. Tying all four horses together, he led them up the slope, arriving as Parker finished his fifth circle looking for tracks.

"I told you there wasn't anything here."

"It's the only snow on the whole goddamn mountain! I saw it. You shot it. It was here." Parker held his arms wide, hat still in his hand.

"Well there's nothing here now, and I don't want to make camp on the cold side of the mountain. You want to move on, or go back where we were?"

Gable did his best to ignore Parker as the man repeatedly spun the cylinder on his revolver and stared out at the purple twilight. The setting sun left behind the false dusk of the Rocky Mountains, holding the night at bay a little longer. They had moved on over the next ridge before making camp, but they had never seen any sign of the buck.

"I still cain't believe that dead deer up and walked away," Parker muttered as he spun the cylinder again.

Gable shook his head in disgust. He was irritated with the clicking sound of Parker playing with the pistol. "You're going to keep worrying at that 'til it bleeds. I missed the shot."

"Then why ain't there no tracks?"

"We went to the wrong place."

"The Hell we didn't!"

Gable spat some loose coffee grounds off the tip of his tongue at the campfire. "Are you going to turn this into some kind of a ghost story? Tell everyone to stay out of these mountains on account of there's a big buck you can't kill lives up here?"

Parker looked sharply up at the big man. "Old Snorter!"

"What?"

"Five years ago, when I come through Cañon City the first time, there was an ol' timer livin' in the bottom of a bottle at the saloon. He tol' story about a big ol' buck called Old Snorter. Said there's a

Spanish gold mine up in the mountains, a cursed one o'course, and it was protected by Old Snorter."

Gable grunted into his coffee tin as he took the last swallow.

"The old man said it couldn't be kilt. Said he shot it four, mebbe five, times, and it would just vanish! Said it was protecting the mine, would show up whenever they got close to it; try to keep 'em away from it." Parker's eyes were wide as he repeated the story. "He said he was the only one of a party of six what made it out alive after finding the cursed mine!"

"Who ever heard of a mule deer protecting anything, let alone a mine?" Gable shook the coffee dregs out of the bottom of his cup, took a bite off his chaw plug, and leaned back on his bedroll.

"Old man said it was some kinda injun magic, a spirit totem, to keep people away. Kept talking 'bout how he wished to God they'd let that buck chase 'em off."

Gable spit into the fire, and listened to the sizzle, trying to ignore Parker's nonsense.

"Wouldn't that be somethin'?" Parker persisted. "If'n we found ourselves an old Spanish gold mine up here? That old man wouldn't talk 'bout no mine though. Alls he kept sayin' was it's cursed."

"You get yourself all spooked, and you're going to have a long night, Parker."

Parker sat up restlessly, holstered his revolver, and poked at the fire. "Would beat the hell out of sellin' hides, for sure. Don't hardly pay nothin' no more. Ain't hardly nothin' up here no more, neither."

A loud cough echoed from somewhere in the forest behind Parker as he finished the words.

Gable chuckled. "There's still something up here."

Parker turned to look into the darkening forest. "Somethin' big, sounds like. Reckon we got a grizzly coming to see what's what?" The wiry man slid out his repeating rifle without taking his eyes off the woods.

"Doubt it. Damn few grizzlies left in Colorado."

Two of the horses snorted nervously. Gable quietly reached out and checked to make sure his Hawken was next to him.

A figure moved silently through the dark trees of the pine forest, a man, barely visible in the night. The man stopped and looked around, as if noticing the campfire for the first time. He snuck closer, staying just out of the firelight. He was a white man, wearing buckskin beaded with intricate patterns by the skilled hand of a squaw. He brought a stubby finger up to his bearded lips, warning Parker and Gable to keep quiet. Then he looked quickly over his shoulder and vanished back into the trees.

Gable slowly pulled back the hammer of his rifle with a quiet click and slunk away from the firelight, towards the nearest tree. He glanced at the horses to see which way their ears were pointed, and focused his attention the same way.

One of the horses snorted and pawed at the ground, and all four began nervously pulling against their tethers.

Parker followed Gable's example and moved away from the firelight, in the opposite direction.

The forest had gone still. The last of the sky darkened and night settled in fully as they waited silently, hearing only the small crackling sounds of the fire. The horses stamped their feet nervously a few times. A long time passed before Parker whispered at Gable.

"I don't see nothin'. You?"

"Cover me," Gable told him, knowing Parker's repeating rifle would protect him better than he could do with his one-shot muzzleloader.

Moving quietly now, unlike tramping through the brush after the deer earlier, Gable circled the campfire, keeping to the shadows and making his way to where the buckskin-clad man had moved through the trees.

The forest was dark, too dark to find any sign of the unknown man's passing, but Gable slinked through the woods like a shadow, first in the direction the man had looked over his shoulder, and then back, following where the man had gone. After finding nothing, he returned to where Parker waited, carefully staying out of the light of the campfire.

"I can't find anything," he told Parker as he settled next to him.

After a long pause staring into the darkness, Parker answered. "I didn't know you was capable of walkin' soft."

"Lot you don't know about me. Reckon we should have killed the fire." Gable worked his way over and kicked dirt over the small flame, smothering it and dropping their world into complete darkness.

"Lot you don't know 'bout me, neither," Parker mumbled back.

A heavy snort, similar to the horses but eerily different, sounded through the forest. Parker turned towards the sound and whispered back to Gable. "Elk?" he asked.

Gable shook his head, not caring Parker couldn't see him, and kept his eyes on the forest, waiting for his night sight to return.

He tensed as he spotted the silhouette of the enormous mule deer staring back at them, its eyes glowing faintly in the starlight. The buck shook his head, threatening them with his antlers. He snorted again, a deep intimidating warning.

Parker fired. The small caliber of his rifle popping three times into the night as Parker worked the pump as fast as he could. The buck vanished.

"Where'd he go?" Parker hissed as he squinted into the darkness, trying to see again. "Goddam it! I know I hit him!"

Gable shook his head, lips pursed as agitation crept over him. Parker shouldn't have been shooting, giving away their position, but even more so, he agreed that Parker had hit the buck. And it had vanished right in front of their eyes.

A strange keening sound reached their ears and Parker stopped his complaining.

"You hear that?" Parker asked hoarsely. "I've heard that sound afore. That's a man. Dying. In a bad bad way." Parker swallowed hard. The little man was visibly shaken

Gable didn't answer. He recognized the sound, too. He didn't know where Parker had heard it, but he had seen the Apache torture a man to death when he was a boy—and it had sounded like that.

A light flickered through the trees in the direction of the horrible sound, and voices followed it.

"I'm mighty glad you put out that fire." Parker's whispered voice, harsh and dry, trembled with fear. "That sounds like injuns."

"They heard the shots. They know where we are." Gable answered. "It's too goddam dark to try to get out of here." He started fumbling in the dark, finding his reloading kit for his Hawken and the spare cartridges for his Colt. "We might have to make a stand for it. How many shots you got left?"

"She holds fifteen, and I only shot three? So's ... I got a lot."

"We need to time it so that you and I are never re-loading at the same time. Keep count on your shots, let me know when you only got two left, so I can cover while you reload."

Parker was silent for a moment. "I ain't so good with countin'."

"With your sidearm, you've still got eighteen. Let me know when you switch guns, so I can help you count. Get yourself ready to reload fast."

The light in the trees continued to move closer, but the voices were indistinct as ever. Angry mumbles and unintelligible words floated through the night. Men's voices. The rustles, rattles, and clanks of their movements told Gable there were many of them, and they weren't Indians.

The agonizing wail that had been constant for the last few minutes cut short with a gurgle. Harsh laughter broke out among the distant voices. The light grew brighter as it approached.

"Get ready," Gable hissed.

Parker swallowed audibly.

Dusky fog lit up in moving beams as the light bobbed through the trees. Shadows of men moved ahead of the light, playing through the beams like ghosts.

"There!" Parker hissed under his breath and pointed his rifle as the first outline came out of the trees—and vanished.

The light went out. The voices stopped.

Gable flinched with his finger on the trigger, nearly firing his weapon. Parker sucked air through his teeth in alarm. One of the horses snorted nervously behind them.

All movement in the forest was gone. The two men sat silent and motionless for a long time, straining their eyes and ears for the men they knew to be in the woods around them, not daring to move or make a sound for fear of giving away their positions.

Cold came with the first light of dawn. Gable finally made out the shadowy shape of Parker, asleep with his face pressed against the bark of a tree. He turned his weary eyes back to the place he'd been staring at all night, where they had last seen the light and the moving figures.

His body was stiff, sore, and cold. The night was a daze in his memory, filled with worry he may not be able to pull the trigger with the finger that had remained frozen in position all night. Still, nothing moved as the forest lightened.

Eventually the birds came to life, flitting in the trees and brush, scratching at the leaves and undergrowth for food. The horses nickered at the coming sun. When two squirrels chased each other through the trees he was watching, Gable finally decided the danger was past.

Parker jerked awake, pointing his rifle around nervously. He spotted Gable and relief melted across his face. He tossed a grin at the big man. "Guess they couldn't find us."

"They didn't look for us."

"How long was I out?"

Gable shrugged. "It was a long night."

Parker rolled off the tree and moaned with stiffness. He looked up towards the brightening sky. "Thank ye, Jesus, for not lettin' those injuns get us."

"It wasn't Indians," Gable began working the kinks out of his body too. "Indians don't wander around the night with lights."

"Then who was it?"

"Damned if I know."

"Lookit this!" Parker waved Gable over. "Lookit up there."

The smaller man pointed up the mountain to a cave entrance, half hidden in the shadows of overhanging rocks. The entrance was squared off and looked to be the work of human hands.

"Maybe we really did find Old Snorter and the Spanish gold mine!" Parker was already pulling at his horse's reigns, trying to lead the way up the slope.

Gable watched him for a moment. "Seems to me you said that it was a *cursed* Spanish gold mine."

"Thought you didn't go in for ghost stories?" Parker grinned over his shoulder as he walked on.

"That was before last night," Gable muttered to himself. He had searched diligently throughout the morning and found no signs of men or of a giant buck he knew had been shot.

He shook his head in resignation and followed Parker upslope, weaving around small piñon trees and buck brush. About halfway up the slope, Gable stopped and looked back. There seemed to be a swath where the growth was different somehow. Almost like a path had been cleared at one time.

Then the white spot caught his eye. A different kind of white than snow, bleached bones always stood out bright against rocks and shrubs. Gable stepped closer to see. Scattered ribs and vertebrae could be hard to tell from for sure, but the broken skull was human.

The day grew hot and still, the air heavy around him. He wiped the sweat from his face with his sleeves and stared at the skull. Bones didn't lie on top of the ground like this for very long until they scatter and break apart.

"Parker!" Gable called, but Parker had reached the cave entrance and paid him no attention. He tried to call again, but his throat had gone dry in the heat and he choked on the sound.

Digging water out of his pack, Gable gulped it quickly, splashing some on his face as he did so. The day had become unbelievably hot.

He leaned on the pack horse and looked around at the trees

lining what he thought might be an old trail. So many of them were dead, they looked like piles of bones, stacked to get them out of the way. He took another drink before putting the water away. He should go see if they really were piles of bones. They looked like bones.

Then he spotted the old pile of leather at the foot of a tree, downhill from the skull. He tied off the horses to a spindly dead branch that reminded him of giant finger bones, and made his way down to see.

The leather, clothing and a pouch, was hard and stiff, caked into one lump from being in the rain and the sun. He flipped the pile over revealing the beaded pattern sewn into it. Some of the beads fell off and bounced down the rocky slope. It was ruined, but recognizable as the same clothing he had seen on the man in the woods the night before. The flap on the pouch cracked and broke as he opened it. Inside was what he would expect to find in any trapper's kit. Reloading patches, balls, and powder horn, some dried up and moldy chaw and jerky, and a few other things, including a ruined newspaper dated 1886.

He looked back at the skull. If the clothes and bag had belonged to the dead man, then the dead man was a white man, and he had been here around five years. And Gable had seen his ghost.

Five years ... The time period stuck in Gable's mind for a moment, then he remembered Parker's story about Old Snorter. Parker had heard it five years ago.

He looked back at the skull. Was this one of the men from Parker's story? One of the men who didn't come back? Had Parker really brought him to an old Spanish gold mine? If so, was it really cursed?

The more he looked up and down the old trail, the more he felt the trees looked like they were made out of bones.

"Woooohooo!" Parker's voice came down the mountain at him. "Lookit this, boy! Goddamned beautiful! Lookit it!"

Gable looked up and spotted Parker doing a slow jig holding up a rock.

"We are goddamned rich!"

Parker moved around the mine entrance like an ant on its hill. The little man's energy was boundless as he scoured through pebbles and rocks, broken remnants dropped by the miners. Some he tossed down the hill, others he sorted into piles. He shoved a few into his pockets, muttering and giggling to himself the whole time. He seemed to have forgotten Gable was even there.

Gable sat quietly, watching, and thinking. He had tried to talk to Parker about the bones on the sides of the trail, but Parker would hear nothing of it. "Just old sticks," Parker had said when Gable had pressed the issue. And the more Gable looked at them, the more he thought maybe Parker was right, but they sure looked like bones.

He had tried to talk about the clothing and the ghost, but Parker had been irritated at being pulled away from the gold by that time, and had ignored that, too.

Perhaps it was the way the trees here felt like giant skeletons watching over him, but while watching Parker, Gable had been grabbed by another notion, and he couldn't let it go.

Parker had damned near walked them straight into this mine, almost as though he knew it was here. He had set Gable up with a story about a mine, just the night before they found it. He had even given explanation, as victims of the curse, for any skeletons they found.

Which, perhaps Parker had known they would.

"We gotta go in!" Parker suddenly stood up and looked around for Gable. "If they left all this gold layin' around out here in the open, imagine what's in there! It must be just fallin' off the walls!"

Parker scurried over to one of the horses and started rummaging in the packs. He came out with a small storm lantern Gable hadn't known was in there. Had Parker known he would need one?

"You comin'?" Parker lit the candle and closed the little metal door on the lamp.

Gable nodded and stood up to follow.

If Parker had killed that man five years ago, and if he intended to kill Gable too, it wouldn't likely be here and now. There must have been some reason for Parker to bring him here. Unless he got greedy for Parker's gold, Gable figured Parker would be wanting to use him to help pack gold out of here, before killing him. Maybe he wanted to find a good place to stash it close to a town, where he could get it himself easy, then he would try to kill Gable.

Following the smaller man into the mine's entrance, Gable kept his distance and tried to stay alert to anything Parker might be up to.

The walls of the mine were roughhewn, work done by the hands of men. The darkness ate up all of the light within ten feet of the mine's mouth. They stopped to let their eyes adjust to the dim candlelight from the small lamp.

The sound of their breathing was heavy in Gable's ears when he heard the clang of metal on rock.

"You hear that?" Parker's whisper was so quiet it was nearly just mouthed.

Gable didn't answer. Could it be Parker had an accomplice? Or maybe someone he thought he had killed, but hadn't, was back to claim the gold for themselves.

"I should go get my rifle." Parker whispered again. "Might be bear, or mountain lion, livin' in here."

Gable bristled at the thought. Then the sound came again, and he was able to pinpoint it. "Or it could be a rat." He pointed further into the cave where a faint gleam could be seen, something reflecting the light back at them. The dark shape of a rodent scampered away from it and into the darkness.

"What's that?" Parker leaned closer without walking forward.

Gable moved nearer to see the silvery thing. "Spanish armor," he told Parker when he got close enough to make it out. Everything about Parker's 'legend' seemed true

He scratched his ear and looked from the breastplate to Parker as he pondered that. Maybe Parker was setting him up for something, but what about the men in the forest, and the vanishing buck? Parker couldn't have done those. Could he? Was there someone else here? Did Parker have an accomplice of some sort? Why the hell would Parker go through all of this trouble?

The dull metallic clank echoed through the mine again, louder this time, and from deeper below. It was not the rat on the armor.

"Knackers?" Parker asked from beside him.

Gable jumped. He hadn't noticed Parker moving closer with the light. The sound had distracted him. He had heard it before; in the night, when the men were walking through the forest. It had been echoed many times, as if all the men were making that sound.

"No. I don't think it's Tommyknockers." He bent down and lightly tapped a fingernail against the breastplate. It sounded with the same flat clunk that came from below.

He thought of the skull outside and the man he had seen in the woods. Had the man's ghost been trying to warn them? Telling them not to disturb the spirits here?

The hair stood up on the back of Gable's neck. This wasn't Parker's doing.

"We have to get out of here," he told Parker. "I think that old man was right. I think this mine is cursed."

Parker wasn't paying attention. He had set the lantern down and was busy examining a rock twice the size of his fist.

"Parker. We have to get out of here."

The clanking sounds increased. There was so much clatter, Gable imagined a legion of Spanish soldiers coming together, getting ready to come marching out. Marching out into the woods by lamplight. That's what they had seen the night before.

"Parker?" Gable put his hand on the man's shoulder.

Parker flinched away from the touch and hissed. "It's mine! Go find your own!"

"We have to get out of here. Now!"

The sounds came closer, growing louder, up out of the hell in the depths of the cave. Parker had no ear for them as he glared at Gable.

"I'm warnin' you! I'm willin' to share the find, but you ain't takin' what's mine! This's gotta be the biggest goddamned nugget anyone ever found!" He clutched the rock close to his chest.

"It's the curse! It's messing with your head. That's nothing but a rock." Gable pointed down into the depths. "They're coming. We have to go."

"Mess with your own head! I don't hear nothin'!"

The sounds grew louder and Gable expected to see the glint of light off metal down in the darkness any second.

"The hell with you." Gable turned and ran back for the glaring light at the tunnel entrance.

"The hell with me? The hell with you!" Parker chased after Gable. "You touch one of those rifles, and I'll kill you first! I'll shoot you in the back if'n I have to!"

He tried to shoulder Gable aside as he passed him. He dropped his rock and it hit another rock, breaking in two. Parker dived for one of the halves and then scrambled to get the other one, glaring at Gable the whole time.

"Parker. Look at the rock. Gold don't break like that. This place is messing with you."

"Just like you and the damned bones, I suppose! You're messin' with me!"

The sounds of voices mixed with the noises coming up from the mine now. Anxious voices. They were hurrying. They were coming for them.

"I'm leaving," Gable told him. "You can keep your 'gold'. I don't want any of it. This place is cursed and I'm getting the hell out of here." He turned and ran out into the sunlight.

Gable stumbled to a stop. The trees had become giant skeletal rib cages and arms, towering over him, reaching for him. He took a step back, out of their reach, back towards the mine and the approaching men.

The horses screamed and pulled at their tethers, snapping the brittle finger bones they had been tied to.

"Damn you, Gable!" Parker yelled and Gable turned to see him running out of the mine as fast as he could with his pistol drawn. He wasn't fast enough.

Soldiers poured out of the darkness, silver armor glinting in the sunlight. Musket fire rang out and Gable felt the bullet rush past his head. He drew his Colt and fired, but the soldiers never slowed. He turned and ran for the horses with Parker chasing after him yelling. More musket fire went by. He felt something hot hit the back of his shoulder and the revolver flew out of his hand. The horse in front of him screamed as a wound opened up in its flank. He grabbed the closest rifle, Parker's repeater, and stumbled backwards, trying to take aim as the soldiers overtook Parker.

He fired as two of them caught up with the little man, their swords flashing as they hacked at him. In an instant, Parker was down, covered with Spanish soldiers who kicked and slashed at him. Gable pumped the rifle and shot again, and again, but there were too many soldiers, he couldn't keep them off Parker.

The horrible keening noise they had heard in the woods the night before started up again, and this time, Gable knew it came from Parker's throat.

Gable fired the rifle blindly into the crowd of armor, pumping it over and over. Soldiers went down, but more kept coming. Gable pumped the action until there were no more shells to be fired. And the soldiers laughed.

They laughed at him as the burning pain in his shoulder finally brought him to his knees, and they closed in slowly around him. One took the reins of Gable's horse, claiming it for his own, laughing as he went through the contents of the saddle bags. Then the soldier leveled a harquebus at him and fired. The old rifle threw off a giant smoke cloud and the impact sent Gable rolling backwards down the hill.

He tried to sit up, but couldn't. He put a hand to his chest, and it came away crimson. Breathing was hard. He looked up into the blue sky and felt the hot sun burning his face. The horrible sound of Parker dying had stopped. He felt a sense of relief that the man wasn't suffering anymore. A movement caught his eye, and he turned his head to look.

The buck stood there, at the edge of the trees, silhouetted by one of the bone piles. It snorted at him and shook its head, flicked its tail, and walked away. Gable thought he could see the shadow of the man who had shushed them following the buck out of sight.

He felt a tear trickling down his cheek. Old Snorter hadn't been protecting the mine after all, he had been trying to warn them. He had been a warning.

"I tol' you, you goddamned ijut!" Parker stumbled down the hill and stood over him, shaking like a leaf. He threw the Hawken rifle on the ground beside Gable. Blood ran from where he had been shot in the arm and the leg. "I tol' you if you touched one of those guns, I'd kill ya!"

"What's with the guy and the rock?" The dusty rider asked after he finished his second drink.

The barkeep looked up from behind the bar and glanced at the small man sitting alone in the corner with the fist sized rock on the table in front of him. The man muttered and mumbled to himself while occasionally turning the rock to look at it differently.

"He don't hurt nothin'."

"I didn't reckon he did. I was just curious why he sits there starin' at that rock."

The barkeep lowered his voice. "He thinks it's a chunk of gold."

The rider raised an eyebrow and looked back at the rock on the table.

"He says it's cursed," the barkeep continued, "and that's why we can't see it's actually gold. He sits there and stares at it all day. He'll tell you a good story if you go ask him about Old Snorter."

The rider laughed. "I got nothin' better to do. I think I'll do that. What's his name?"

"Parker."

The rider placed some money on the bar. "Set me up a drink to take him to pay for the story. I can't figure his cursed gold buys much around her."

Setting a bottle on the bar, the bartender whispered, "If you get him talking, see if you can find out where he got the rock."

"If it's 'cursed' gold, what's it matter?"

The barkeep reached low behind the bar and brought something up. He dropped a few pebbles onto the bar.

The rider leaned in to look close at the tiny golden nuggets. "Because it ain't all cursed."

Victor's Story

The boy was scared. He had been told to expect anything, but he hadn't expected to see four old witches summon up a demon from Hell.

Judging from their reactions, neither had the old women.

He knew it was a demon from Hell because he had seen it. More than that, he had felt, even *tasted*, its vile presence.

Hiding under the old writing desk, he held his knees tight to his chest, clamped there by his arms in a death grip. The knuckles on his hands were white with strain. His breathing was short and quick as his heart pounded in his ears. His eyes flitted uncontrollably, anxiously searching through the darkness of the room. Finding nothing else, they reflected only his fear.

The noises in the kitchen had stopped a long time ago, but he knew it was not over. He had listened to the old woman sobbing in the darkness for a long time but he hadn't been able to bring himself to go to her. Finally, her crying had faded until he could no longer hear it, and he was ashamed of himself for not going to help, but fear prevented him from giving up his hiding place. He spent a long time trying not to cry.

It had all started with something resembling a séance but had quickly turned into a horror movie. When the demon's small form coalesced on the center of the table in front of the women, he had been mesmerized by the evil it exuded. He had *felt* it searching for something and when the feeling passed, it was like greasy fingers leaving slimy snail-trails on his soul. The demon's attentions had left slowly, slithering palpably away from him, seeming to flow backwards into the rapidly appearing body of the demon and becoming part of the hideously putrid smelling vapors that slowly dissipated into the air around the tiny creature on the kitchen table.

Panting with fear, the boy now looked out from his hiding place into the dark room, wishing he was anywhere but here. He wasn't sure what had happened. The old women had spoken only in Spanish, unless they were talking to him, and he only really knew the curse words he had picked up from his friends.

He said a Hail Mary and crossed himself. He had never actually paid attention to the words before, but now that he really wanted the prayer to work, he found himself listening to the words as he whispered them silently under his breath.

"Hail Mary, full of grace, the lord is with thee; blessed art thou among women and blessed is the fruit of thy womb, Jesus. Holy Mary, Mother of God, pray for us now, and at the hour of our death, Amen." It helped. Not a lot, but it did help.

At first, the words didn't really seem appropriate for the situation, but the more he muttered them, the more fitting they seemed to become. He was going to die. The demon was going to find him. He knew from the oily touch against his soul that the demon wanted nothing more than it wanted him. He knew it would come back for him.

He muttered the prayer again, and again, just as had heard his mother do when she was upset. He said the words so fast he wasn't even sure what he was saying anymore, but it helped. It seemed to clear away the nasty, grimy coating the foul smell had left in his mouth, but it didn't help the filthy, filmy feeling left on his skin.

After what seemed a long time, he felt he might regain control of his body again. His heart was staying where it was supposed to, and his breathing came easier, although it still caught in his throat occasionally. His eyes slowly began seeing again instead of endlessly searching the dark. He released his grip on his knees and flexed his outstretched fingers to ease the pain. Crawling out from under the desk headfirst, he found his legs had lost feeling.

He moved cautiously, soundlessly as he could, listening for any signs of the demon's tiny clicking hooves on the kitchen tile in the other room. When he was finally able to stretch out, he sat on the floor in the darkness and waited for his legs to return to the land of the living, wincing as tiny needle pains pricked the bottom of his feet and up and down both legs.

His eyes were transfixed on the doorway back into the kitchen, searching for any sign the demon might return. The guttering candlelight from the kitchen was dimmer than before; some of the candles must have gone out. He felt he was peeking through a flickering doorway into the gates of Hell. He listened for the sobbing of the old woman, but still heard nothing.

He wondered if any of the four old women were left. At the instant the demon had appeared the first one had fainted or maybe even died, he wasn't sure which. Involuntarily glancing around the drawing room quickly, he kept checking for lurking shadows, remembering how the demon had immediately lashed out with a disproportionately long arm and struck down the second woman.

She had flown across the room and landed against the wall in a heap. The sound of her limp body hitting the wall and dropping to the floor stuck oddly in his mind, as if it had been the only sound made. The demon itself had made no noise other than the dull thud of its gnarled hand striking the old woman. He thought she was probably dead and, though he could see her in his peripheral vision, he refused to look towards that corner as he began crawling into the kitchen.

His legs felt better but fear still prevented him from standing upright, sending shivers of weakness through his body that caused his hands to tremble and his knees to shake. Slowly, on his hands and knees as best he could, he crawled across the cold tile kitchen floor, making his way towards the door he had seen the third old woman run through.

Crawling around spilled wax and sputtering flames, he remembered how the demon scattered the candles as it had leaped after the fleeing woman. With tiny vestigial bat-wings flapping futilely on its back, it had hit the floor with its split hooves sharply clicking on the tiles as it scrabbled for purchase. The creature stood upright on backwards-bending horse legs, giving it great strength for leaping once its hooves finally found purchase in the grout between the tiles. It stood less than two feet tall, with a face between that of dog and a horse; long, with the eyes on the sides of its head.

The boy wondered at how something so small could be so strong and feared he might have glimpsed fangs under the curling snarl of its lips.

He had been standing near the corner of the room, far from the demon when it bounded off the table. The fourth old lady had quickly grabbed something long and silvery from a shelf and determinedly chased after the demon and the other woman. She was one he had been told to call 'Abulea,' and was also the one he thought he had heard sobbing. She was his great-grandmother, but he really didn't know her at all.

When paralyzing terror finally lost out to the instinct to survive, he had run into the study and folded himself under the desk. Muffled

43

noise had come from beyond the far door, but he had not dared to imagine what was happening on the other side of those walls. He had heard two or three more muffled thumps followed by an oppressive silence, and then the quiet sobbing had begun. He stayed hidden and listened to it for a long time.

When the crying finally faded, the silence had been complete again. He had only the memory echoes of various muffled sounds to keep him company. The entire incident had seemed to take place with an unnatural quiet, as though the world had been covered with cotton.

Now, still on his hands and knees, he reached the threshold of the door the demon had passed through. His mouth was dry and sticky as he slowly peered around the edge of the doorframe. Dim candlelight flickered tauntingly out into the room through his doorway, pretending to reveal what lie in the darkness.

His heart stuttered at a movement until he recognized it was his own shadow wavering in the weak candlelight. After a moment his eyes adjusted enough to discern two forms; one in the middle of the room and the other against the far wall. He was sure these were the old women and that they would be dead now, but the wavering light cast the illusion of movement over everything making it hard to tell for sure.

He sniffed at the air and found the taste of dank rotten garbage that had exuded from the demon. He wondered if the smell meant the demon was still here or if it had permeated the room the same way it had filled his own senses and covered his skin. He hoped it was just leftover stink.

Crawling towards the shadowy forms, his palm landed on something cold and hard. He fumbled silently with it in the dark. It glinted with the cold silvery reflection of metal. He drew a sharp breath of pain when he discovered the object to be some sort of knife. He brought his stabbed finger to his mouth and tasted the buttery flavor of his own blood. The cut stung, but it was not bad enough to worry about right now.

He turned the knife over in his hands and held it blade out for a moment. It was awkwardly shaped and hard to clutch as a weapon, but he was comforted nonetheless. He turned his newfound weapon over in his hand and pointed the blade out of the bottom of his palm as he had seen the older kids say was the proper way to wield a knife. It was uncomfortable to hold while crawling. Gripping it while moving ground his knuckles into the hard floor and he worried about stabbing himself in the knee, but he was afraid holding it wrong would make it useless.

He thought this knife might have been what he had seen his grandmother grab on her way out of the kitchen. If it was, she hadn't made it very far into this room with it.

He held his breath for a moment and listened for any noise. He thought that perhaps he could hear one of the women breathing lightly, maybe wetly, as if she was congested.

He could tell the woman closest to him was his grandmother. The candlelight was dim here, and the colors were washed out, but his grandmother's red-checkered apron was easily discernable. He continued towards her, pausing his own breathing often so he could listen into the silence better.

When he reached his grandmother, he put his hand to her face to see if he could feel any breathing. Her breath was shallow and slight, but it was there. He didn't see anything wrong with her, other than she wasn't moving, but she was very old and he had seen how hard the demon had hit the other old woman at the table.

He could still hear the moist breathing sound from before, and it wasn't from his grandmother. Maybe the other woman was still alive. He decided he wouldn't check on her. He would try to get outside and go for help instead. What did he know about helping someone who had been attacked by a demon? He wasn't even sure he could find his way back to his aunt's house where the rest of his family was, but he could certainly get a neighbor or someone to help.

He resumed crawling towards the far side of the room. He knew the front door was there, somewhere in the dark. The old women had closed all the doors and windows to keep out the prying eyes of gossiping neighbors. The only other way out of the house was through the back door into the courtyard, but the courtyard had eight-foot walls and the boy knew the gate was padlocked. The front door was the only way out.

He sensed movement and froze. His eyes began searching through the misleading flickers of the candlelight for the source of the movement. It came from the other old woman. Maybe she was waking up. He decided that maybe he should check on her after all. If she was waking up, she could help the others, besides she was only a few feet away. He switched the knife to his other hand and pivoted silently on one knee to face the old woman.

He stared hard at the dim lump of her form, trying to make out any details. She was on her left side with her back towards him. He thought the movement had come from her right arm where perhaps she had moved her hand to her face. He inched closer putting his every effort into being silent, the horror of the demon still strong in his memory. He still held his breath to make sure he could hear over his own noises. The breathing sound was louder now, but it sounded wrong, like someone softly blowing bubbles with a straw.

Another movement. He froze. He had seen the movement this time. It looked like maybe the woman was scratching her chin, but he hadn't seen her arm move. He raised his head a little higher to see over her. There was definitely some movement.

Whatever it was, it didn't look right to him. He felt his pulse quicken again. He changed his mind about going to the woman. He moved his knees backwards away from the old woman in a reverse crawl. The knife-thing in his hand scraped the floor.

The demon's head popped up from behind the woman's form. He froze. He was able to see it clearly as its beady black eyes locked onto his. The eyes reminded him of a mouse's eyes: protruding, hard, shiny, and completely inhuman. Flickering candlelight reflected in them like the burning pits of Hell. Gruesomely shaped, the head was like that of a rat, a horse, and a dog. The mouth showed barred teeth and fangs glinting orange in the darkness. The boy had no doubts the dark wet stain around the demon's muzzle was blood.

Caution was lost in the face of discovery. The boy lurched into a standing position. The demon leapt at him. There was no time to escape. Reflexively he threw up his hands to protect his face and to swat away the attack of the cat-sized creature.

It was a futile effort. The weight of the demon hit the boy as hard as a full-grown man. The boy was propelled backwards over a chair and coffee table. He felt things breaking. He wasn't sure if it was the chair, the table, or his own bones. The weight of the demon sat on his chest like a bag of cement. Its fetid, putrid smell of rotting eggs and burnt hair suffocated him as much as the burden of the demon on his chest. He felt its gnarled and clawed hands rake down the side of his face, as its wiry legs kicked sharp hooves into his abdomen and thighs. The boy gasped in pain so intense he couldn't cry out. He squeezed his eyes shut tight in a grimace as fierce as the demon's and waited for the end to come.

The weight of the demon felt as if it was slowly lifted away and the pain began to fade into dull throbs. The boy wondered at the strange sensations of death. He had always been told it would be painless, but he had expected the pain to stop suddenly, not fade away. He took a deep breath and was rewarded with a stabbing pain in his side. He convulsed and rolled up, clutching his side and causing more pain. He gasped and fought to breathe without using his chest. The pain was worse than ever as he clutched his side involuntarily.

He opened his eyes, surprised to be alive, and spun around, fearful of the demon. He nearly passed out from the agony of movement. There was no sign of the demon anywhere. He fumbled about in the broken pieces of wood and glass from the coffee table. Had he fainted? He didn't think so.

He still had the knife-thing clutched tightly in his grasp. It was slick in his grip and coated with something. Blood, maybe. Maybe it was his. He hurt in too many places to know how bad he was bleeding. He could now tell the knife was some sort of ornate cross-shaped dagger or letter opener that had been sharpened. He held it up in front of him again, ready for another attack.

Blood was flowing into his eyes and obscuring his vision. He could feel hot wet liquids on his shirt and legs. There was movement behind him again. He wheeled about in desperation and wiped at the blood in his eyes. He tripped and fell back, sprawling into the pile of glass and wooden shards. A light clicked on and the room was suddenly too bright to see anything.

The boy shielded his eyes from the light, trying to hold the dagger at ready, but the pain in his side and his position on the ground prevented it.

"It's okay," came a hoarse and thickly accented voice. He searched the blinding glare for the voice, waving the knife out into the air, trying to turn to protect himself.

"It's okay." The voice repeated. "It's gone now."

The boy finally recognized the voice. It was the old lady the demon sent flying against the wall. She was leaning heavily against the doorframe, her hand still on the light switch.

The boy looked from her to the knife in his trembling hand and saw it was covered with something slick and black, like tar colored pond scum. Dropping his weapon, he closed his eyes and laid his head back into the broken glass. He thought that maybe he would like to faint now.

Instead, he allowed himself to drift off slowly, mentally keeping time with the pain throbbing in his leg, ribs and face. He smiled as he imagined they were a little like the bass drums he had seen in a parade once, beating so low you felt them in your chest as much as you heard them. He was comforted by the sound and feel of the drums as he heard the woman say it was okay again.

It wasn't okay. He didn't think it would ever be okay again, but just for right now, the drums were very nice.

Author's Note

Victor's Story is part of the back story, and prologue, for *Lucid Nightmares*, a novel I wrote in 2010. *Lucid Nightmares* was for sale, for a brief time, as an e-book, but was taken down at the request of a small publisher I was working with. They were interested in the novel, and did not want a competing edition on the market. I couldn't blame them, so I took it down. Three years and three small publishers later, it is still not available. But it will be. Soon.

Support Independent Artists

Things are different now. Things are changing, and we need your help. Independent artist's books won't be found in a bookstore or a supermarket. It's all we can do to get on Amazon or Barnes and Noble. Please, rate us, review us, tell others about us. Go to Amazon, B&N, Goodreads, Kobo, Smashwords, or anywhere else you like to look for books, and tell us, and everyone else, what you thought about our books. Please be honest. Review the book, don't bash the author or make irrelevant statements. Don't accept pirated copies. Don't buy pirated copies. Why give money to the thief and put an author you like out of business? Most authors make very little money and work as a labor of love (truth be told, most authors never turn a profit). Tell your friends about the books you like. Support the authors you want to see more from. Blog about them. Tweet and Facebook about them. Ask your library and local bookstore to carry their books. In the age of the internet, the reader -YOU- have the power to make or break an author. Really. One person could do it. Use it. Use that power well, and use it responsibly.

If you read one of my books, and you review/rate it, let me know, and I will send you a short story to thank you. Just be honest with your review. You can reach me at sam@samknight.com. Thank you for your support.

–Sam Knight

Why I Write

This post originally appeared on <u>The Fictorians</u> *blog on May 4, 2013. This is a question I get asked often, especially after people find out how much money most writers DON'T make. Most of us never break even on the costs of putting ourselves out there, and even the better known authors make only a moderate income. Yeah, I know, J.K. Rowling, Stephen King ... Those are people who won the lottery. Actually winning the lottery is easier. According to sources I won't admit to quoting because I don't trust the internet, there are 1,600 $1 million or more lottery winners every year. How many big name authors can you name?*

The next time you read a 'review' of a book that is nothing but slander against the author, please remember to take that into account before you allow someone else to pass judgment for you.

My grandfather and my mother are avid readers, so I came by that honestly. Writing however is a different story.

I have a tendency to get sick. I mean really sick. If everyone else in the house has a sniffle, I have a cold. If they have colds, I have the flu. If everyone has the flu, I'm at the doctor's. The problem with getting that sick, that often, is you get bored really stinking fast.

Being a child in the 70's, I didn't have video games until Pong came out, and I could play that for only so long. Television was only worth watching for about two hours a day, and then only on some days (except Saturday morning cartoons!). Books though ... they worked 24/7.

One particular illness sticks out in my memory. I was in fifth grade and down sick with what I was told was the 'Russian Flu.' I was miserable sick –except when I was reading. When I was reading, I was in another world. I could literally forget about my own problems! I would be so engrossed, the rest of the world ceased to exist. That was a godsend.

That was also my first real introduction to the idea of a 'series' where the story continued on into the next book. The world didn't come to an end when I closed the book, there was another one waiting!

I read Patricia A. McKillip's Riddle Master Trilogy, Piers Anthony's Xanth Trilogy (back when there were only three), a trilogy collection of Edgar Rice Burroughs' John Carter books, and three or four of Alan Dean Foster's Pip and Flinx series. When I ran out of new books, I re-read The Hobbit.

It was quite an eclectic mix, and I read them all in a little over a week. And then I went looking for more. Everything I could get my hands on. Up until that time, I had been a 'reader'. I had read the Hobbit and The Lord of the Rings in Fourth grade. But now, after doing so much reading, so intensively, I had become addicted. I had become a biblioholic. I had to have more!

I raided my mother's bookshelves and then I headed for my grandfather's. I came away with armloads of Andre Norton, Robert Heinlein, Kenneth Robeson, Frank Herbert, and more.

Some sucked me in, other's not so much. I was searching for authors with a specific talent –the ability to make me forget I was reading a book. I was actually trying to recreate what I had experienced while I was ill.

Yeah, I read the things the other kids were reading. The Mouse and the Motorcycle, Charlie and the Chocolate Factory, and the like. They were good, but… they didn't transport me into another world the way I wanted.

I wasn't in the game to read about little problems with kid brothers, or mysteries about missing toys. I wanted the Hero's Journey. I wanted books that let me see Star Wars in my head. (We couldn't just buy it and watch it anytime we wanted back then. Not to mention that, if I remember right, Star Wars was around $100 when it came out on VHS five or six years after theatrical release, and a brand new book was only $3.50.) I wanted books that let me live a different life.

And I found them. I found a lot of them. I started with authors I already knew could make a movie behind my eyes, and I got everything I could by them. I read Piers Anthony's older sci-fi stories, and then I followed all of his new series as they came out. I followed Alan Dean Foster's Pip and Flinx adventures all the way until 2009 when he finally wrapped it up. I'm still waiting for David Gerrold to finish The War Against the Chtorr series (not holding my breath though…) Along the way, I found Robert Asprin's Myth series, Lawrence Watt-Evan's Ethshar books, Terry Pratchett's Discworld, and more.

I worked 60 hours a week while attending college full time, and I still made time to read. I would exchange books with co-workers. I gave away my copy of Douglas Adams' Hitchhiker's Guide to the Galaxy just to convince someone to read it, and then I went and bought myself another. I did that three times.

After I graduated, I carried my book du jour to work with me and read it during my lunch hour. At first my new co-workers laughed at me, but by the time I left there were close to a dozen people doing the same thing.

Why? Because books are magic. A well-crafted book made by a talented author will cast a spell over a reader and transport them to a new place, a different time, another life.

That's what I was looking for when I was sick. A different life. And those wonderful authors gave it to me, even if it was just for stolen moments at a time. They gave it to me. And as I lay in that bed so many years ago, a thought drifted through my mind. A thought that stayed with me the rest of my life.

I wanted to return the favor. I wanted to write something that could bring as much joy to those authors as they were giving me.

Ideas began bouncing around in my head after that. When I worked physical labor, I would entertain myself by thinking up stories. When I drove long distance, I would stay awake by imagining new places, new worlds, and new people. Eventually, I found that nearly anything would give me a story idea.

And soon, very soon, I will finally move beyond my apprenticeship and craft a story that repays my heroes. I will inspire the next generation, and honor the previous. I will write because I read, and it was wonderful.

Author Biography

Photo by Stacey Vowell

A Colorado native, Sam Knight spent ten years in California's wine country before returning to the Rockies. When asked if he misses California he gets a wistful look in his eyes and replies he misses the green mountains in the winter, but he is glad to be back home.

His grandfather and mother are avid readers and Sam says his own passion started when he pressed his grandfather to find out what was so interesting. His grandfather handed him a book and he has been an avid reader ever since. He claims to have finished the Hobbit and the Lord of the Rings trilogy in fourth grade and says he can still remember the look, feel, and smell of some of those early books. (He has been spotted sniffing books as he ruffles the pages.)

While doing research for a Western novel, Sam was not surprised to find out that, once upon a time, half of his family had been on the wrong side of the law. It stands to reason that when your great-great-grandfather was a marshal in Cripple Creek, Colorado, someone in the family had to be a horse thief. Sam was, however, surprised to find the family name had originally been McKnight and that the thieves had taken the 'Mc' part of the name with them. (Or the lawmen let them have it to distance themselves from that side of the family.) Having served a stint working in a correctional facility, he has often wondered if being a lawman runs in the blood. His great grandfather upheld the law in Mooreland, OK, as well as Springfield and Florence CO, among other places, with his grandfather occasionally deputized to assist.

When asked why he would want to become a writer, Sam recounts a time when he was in fifth grade. Illness stuck him in bed for two weeks with only books for companions. (This was a bit before video game phone implants were in common use.) He burned through the Xanth trilogy (back before it expanded into thirty some books), the Riddle of Stars trilogy, a couple of John Carter of Mars books, and several Pip and Flinx novels, relishing the moments when he would become so engrossed he would forget the ills of the physical. A thought floated through his mind at that time, about being able to return the favor to the authors who were providing so much to him. That thought never left and now he sincerely hopes anyone picking up one his stories can find something they were looking for.

Drop in and see what he is up to at SamKnight.com. If you have something you want to say, leave a comment, or contact him at sam@samknight.com

Author Bibliography

Published by Knight Writing Press:
Four Adventure!
Time Travel Trio

Stories in anthologies available now:
The Maltese Dragon
Captain Samjack's Terror Emporium

Stories a little bit harder to find:
The Copper Colored Hummingbird
The Cat Lady and the Dragon
A Small Town Santa

Things that are *Free*:
Broken (A Flash Fiction Piece)
Boutonnière (A Flash Fiction Piece)
Steam Punk Nursery Rhymes

Coming Soon:
A Whiskey Jack in a Murder of Crows
Lucid Nightmares Part 1: Bedeviled

Links to find or purchase can be found on the author's website:

SamKnight.com

Are You Still Reading This Stuff?

A reward for your dedication!

A free short story can be found on my website at: samknight.com/?page_id=1270.

The name of the story is Catching the Dead Eye Special.

I entered the NYC Midnight 2013 Short Story Challenge, going up against more than 800 other writers. (I didn't win.) For this competition, I was assigned to write a story, 2,500 words or less, within the following guidelines: Genre: Horror, Subject: a flight on a private jet, Character: a drug dealer. I had less than a week to do it. Some have suggested that I needed to turn this into a much longer story to do it justice. Come visit my website, read the story, and let me know what you think in the comments section.